T0381038

African Folktales from my Childhood

ALIEH KIMBENG

Balboa Press books may be ordered through booksellers or by contacting:

Balboa Press
A Division of Hay House
1663 Liberty Drive
Bloomington, IN 47403
www.balboapress.com
844-682-1282

Interior Image Credit: Kimbeng Nde-Mukong Ricky

ISBN: 978-1-9822-6381-2 (sc)
ISBN: 978-1-9822-6387-4 (e)

Library of Congress Control Number: 2021902789

Print information available on the last page.

Balboa Press rev. date: 03/03/2021

Contents

Acknowledgments

Big thanks to my father, Mr. Kimbeng Richard Nde Nche, Grandma, Dr. Ivo Ditah, Francis Ditah, Quinta Ditah, Schneider Kimbeng, and Mambo Che for taking the time to tell me these stories. I want to thank Phaedra Beckwith and Gretchen Hansen for looking over my first draft and giving me feedback. I would also like to thank my incredibly talented younger brother, Kimbeng Nde-Mukong Ricky, who did all the illustrations. This book could not have been brought to life without him. Lastly, I would like to thank my family, friends, and everyone who supported me during this process.

Tales of John and Mary

John, Mary, and the Hunter

Once upon a time, in the Kingdom of Mankondelle, there lived twins named John and Mary. Some said they were the prettiest twins in the world. Mary had beautiful dark skin, a big afro which she always let free, and a smile that could light up any room. John looked like his sister in every way except he had cornrow braids. *(Cornrow is a hair braiding style in which hair is braided very close to the scalp, using an underhand, upward motion to make a continuous, raised row.)*

Despite their physical similarities, they were very different. John was stubborn, didn't do well in school, and always got into trouble. On the other hand, Mary did well in school, obeyed her parents, and rarely got into trouble. One day, John and Mary's parents asked them to fetch flowers, stating that the person who brought back the prettiest flowers would get something special. John and Mary went separately to fetch the flowers, but they ran into each other on their way home. When John saw Mary's flowers, he became extremely jealous because her flowers were prettier than his. He tried to trade with Mary, telling her that his flowers were better than hers, but she refused.

John really wanted the special gift from their parents, so when he realized that Mary wasn't going to let him have her flowers, he killed her, buried her under a tree, and took her flowers home. When he got home, he told his parents that he didn't know where Mary was. His parents believed him because, after all, they had left separately to fetch the flowers. John's mom was happy with the flowers he had brought home, so she decided to make him his favorite meal; water fufu and eru. During dinner, Mary's parents were worried about her because it was getting late, and she had never missed dinner. So, after dinner, they decided to search for Mary. When they couldn't find her, they asked some of their neighbors to help in the search. They searched the entire night, but no one could find Mary. The whole neighborhood was so worried that they alerted the Fon *(A ruler of a tribe)*. He sent out more people to look for Mary, but they still couldn't find her.

A few weeks later, a hunter from the Kingdom was on his way home when he stopped to rest under the tree where John had buried Mary. When he sat under the tree, Mary's bones started singing.

"Hunter man, hunter man, don't touch my bones. My brother killed me in the bush and took my flowers home, oh chingmalinga chingmalinga, ching, ching, ching, ching."

The hunter was startled, so he stood up quickly but decided to sit under the tree again to confirm what he had just heard. When he sat under the tree, Mary's bones sang.

"Hunter man, hunter man, don't touch my bones. My brother killed me in the bush and took my flowers home, oh chingmalinga chingmalinga, ching, ching, ching, ching."

The hunter decided to find the singing bones' family, so he dug them up and took them to the palace. When he arrived at the palace, he told the Fon the story. The Fon did not believe him, so the Fon decided to step on the bones. When the Fon stepped on the bones, they started singing.

"Fon, Fon, don't touch my bones. My brother killed me in the bush and took my flowers home, oh chingmalinga chingmalinga, ching, ching, ching, ching."

The Fon was amazed, so he gathered all the villagers to find what family the bones belonged to. One by one, the villagers stepped on the bones, and it sang the same song, calling out the person's name.

When it was John's turn, he didn't want to step on the bones because he already knew who they belonged to, but his parents and the Fon forced him. When John finally stepped on the bones, they sang.

"John, John, don't touch my bones. You killed me in the bush and took my flowers home, oh chingmalinga chingmalinga, ching, ching, ching, ching."

The entire village was speechless and couldn't believe that John had committed such an atrocity. The Fon ordered the Chindas *(A palace servant or guard)* to give John 100 lashes and kill him.

Moral of the story: If you steal flowers, they may be used to decorate your grave.

John, Mary, and Jollof Rice

Once upon a time, in the Kingdom of Mankondelle, there lived twins named John and Mary. Some said they were the prettiest twins in the world. Mary had beautiful dark skin, a big afro which she always let free, and a smile that could light up any room. John looked like his sister in every way except he had cornrow braids.

On the last day of school, John and Mary's mother cooked a big pot of Jollof rice *(A popular rice dish eaten across many West African countries)* before she went to the farm.

When John and Mary received their report cards, Mary took first place while John failed, so he had to repeat the class. John wasn't bothered; all he cared about was the Jollof rice that his mother had cooked, so he ran home ahead of Mary and ate all the Jollof.

When he finished eating, he covered the pot and left the house. When Mary got home, she opened the pot, hoping to get some Jollof, but it was empty. As she was closing the pot, John walked in and asked her what she was doing. She told him she had just gotten home and wanted to eat, but there was no food. Mary was very hungry, so she went to the neighbor's house, hoping to get something to eat. In the evening, their parents came home hungry and were surprised that there was no jollof rice left. They asked John and Mary who ate all the Jollof, and John said that Mary ate it because she got home before him. Mary denied it and started crying. To find the truth, their parents decided to take them to the Mami Wata *(a water spirit venerated in West, Central, Southern Africa, and the African diaspora in the Americas.)*

The Mami Wata is a water spirit who knows everything, so no one can lie to her.

When they got to the river, John and Mary's parents explained why they were there. The Mamiwata told them that the person who ate the Jollof would not leave the river alive, so this is their last chance to tell the truth. Even after hearing this, John still maintained his innocence. The Mami Wata told everyone to step further into the river and sing this song. *"If na me chop that rice, if na me chop that rice, oh cover pot go cover me, oh Mamiwater go swallow me, chachum, chachum."* When everyone finished singing the song, a cover pot came up from the river and covered John then the Mami Wata swallowed him. Mary and her parents went home and never saw John again.

Moral of the story: Dishonesty and death are next-door neighbors.

John and Mary's Gifts

Once upon a time, in the Kingdom of Mankondelle, there lived twins named John and Mary. Their father was the best hunter in the village, so they always had an abundance of meat, which they ate with everything. One day, some Europeans came to the village and started cutting down trees for timber. This caused all the animals to lose their homes, and some of them died.

Due to the deforestation, there were no longer any animals for the hunter to hunt. This troubled the hunter's wife because they ate everything with meat. One day, John and Mary overheard their parents talking about the shortage of meat, and their mother asked if she could kill one of the kids for meat. Their father was furious at the suggestion because they had prayed for years before their ancestors blessed them with kids. When John and Mary heard this, they were afraid for their lives. The next day when everyone had left the house, John and Mary's mother cut off one of her breasts and used it to cook Fufu Corn and NjamaNjama. In the evening, when everyone returned home, they were so happy to see meat on the table. While they were eating, John asked his mother where she had gotten the meat. She just opened her shirt and showed him.

John, Mary, and their father were shocked and couldn't believe what they had just seen. They threw up and tried to get all the food out of their stomach. After dinner, John and Mary planned their escape just in case they were next on their mother's list for meat. At midnight when everyone was asleep, John and Mary packed their things and left.

They didn't know where they were going, so they walked for days and nights, through sunshine and rain, hoping to find another village. One day while Mary was sleeping under a tree, she dreamt that her ancestors came to her and said, "When you cry, it will rain. When you smile, the sun will shine. When you put your feet in water, all the fishes will die and come up. And when you comb your hair, gold will fall".

When Mary woke up, she immediately told John about her dream. He was very excited, so he told her to try everything their ancestors had told her in the dream. They went to a river, and Mary put her feet in it; all of a sudden, dead fishes started surfacing in the river.

They were so happy; They made a fire, cooked the fish, and ate it. In order to try the next gift, John had to make Mary cry. As Mary was crying, the heaviest rain they had ever seen started falling, so John begged her to stop crying.

When Mary stopped crying, John made her smile. When she started smiling, the sun came out, which helped dry their clothes. They were in disbelief, so Mary decided to try the last gift by combing her beautiful afro. As Mary combed her hair, it increased in length, and gold fell on the ground.

They were so happy, so they continued walking, hoping to find a village nearby. After a few hours of walking, they arrived at a road with two paths and didn't know which one to take when they saw a little frog. They asked the frog which direction to take. The frog told them that the path to the left led to a very wealthy village, but the inhabitants were not hospitable. Whereas the path to the right led to a poor village with very hospitable people.

John and Mary thanked the frog and decided to go to the poor village. When they arrived at the poor village, they met a very kind old lady. Mary asked the old lady if they could stay with her because they had nowhere else to go. The old lady agreed to let them stay for as long as they needed. The old lady treated them like her own children. After a few weeks of living with the old lady, her kindness led John and Mary to trust her, so they told her about Mary's gifts. The old lady didn't believe them, so Mary decided to show her by combing her beautiful afro. As Mary combed her hair, gold fell on the ground. The old lady was shocked and immediately went on her knees to thank her ancestors for blessing her through John and Mary. John and Mary agreed to start paying the old lady in gold for food and shelter. Due to the gold the old lady was receiving, she started buying herself expensive things. Her neighbors began noticing the changes in her life, and gossip began spreading across the village.

As time went by, the old lady became jealous of Mary's gifts and wanted the gifts for herself, so she went to a medicine man who told her that she needed to hurt or kill Mary to have the gifts. *(a medicine man is a traditional healer or spiritual leader)* Unbeknown to John and Mary, the old lady started plotting to harm Mary. One day, when John went to fetch firewood, the old lady asked Mary to accompany her to the valley to harvest some rare herbs. When they got close to the valley, the old lady blew a powder on Mary's face, which made her weak. She then removed Mary's eyes and threw her into the valley, hoping she will die.

21

The old lady then sold Mary's eyes to a hunter for a big bag of rice. Later that evening, when John got home, he started looking for Mary but couldn't find her. He asked the old lady, but she said she didn't know where Mary was. News had also gotten to the Queen about Mary's gifts, and she felt threatened. The Queen sent a servant to the old lady's house to tell John and Mary to come to the palace in four days and showcase Mary's gifts. When the servant gave John the message, he was afraid because his sister was missing, and he only had four days to find her. John continued to search for Mary to no avail. The old lady pretended to search too and comforted John.

While in the valley, Mary started crying and it started raining like it had never rained before. Everyone in the village was surprised because it was the heart of the dry season. As Mary drew closer to death, she started singing and calling on her ancestors to help her. A hunter was on his way back home when he heard Mary singing. Her voice was so beautiful, so he followed the sound until he found her.

When the hunter found Mary, he felt sorry for her, so he gave her some food and water. When Mary finished eating, the hunter took her to his house, where she told him her story. Mary didn't know that she was talking to the same hunter whom the old lady had sold her eyes. When Mary finished telling the hunter her story, he took the eyes he had bought from the old lady and put them in Mary's eye sockets.

The eyes fit perfectly, and Mary could see again. To thank the hunter, Mary combed her hair and gave him gold. After she gave him the gold, she asked him to help her find her brother. It was the day John had to report to the palace, and he had not yet found Mary. The Queen sent guards to the old lady's house to arrest John and put him in jail because she thought he was hiding Mary.

After John's arrest, the old lady went to the valley to ensure that Mary was dead, but she didn't find Mary. The old lady was furious and continued to search for Mary to kill her. News of John's arrest reached Mary and the hunter, so they ran to the palace and tried talking to the Queen, but the guards refused to let them in. After three hours of struggling and trying to convince the guards, the Queen agreed to talk to them. Mary told the Queen that she was John's sister and would do anything to get him released. The Queen told her to come back the next day so that all the villagers would be present to see her gifts. When Mary left, the Queen sent servants to every household, inviting them to the palace. The next day, Mary arrived the party with her hair in a bun wearing a beautiful gold dress.

Towards the end of the party, the Queen announced that she had a special guest who claims to have gifts from the ancestors that no one had ever seen. The Queen then ordered Mary to come to the center and humiliated her until she cried. As Mary cried, it started raining heavily. The villagers were starting to believe that Mary had gifts, but the Queen dismissed it, saying that the rain was only a coincidence. The Queen then ordered Mary to smile. As Mary smiled, the sun came out even though it was past midnight. All the villagers, including the Queen, were astonished, and they finally believed Mary. Mary asked the Queen to release John because she had proven that she has gifts. The Queen refused and told her that she would be executed at dawn because people like her, and her brother will only bring trouble to the village. Mary begged the Queen and the villagers to let her and her brother go and promised never to return. The Queen refused, so Mary started crying. As Mary cried, heavy rain fell. The villagers felt sorry for Mary, so they all decided to dethrone their Queen and make Mary their Queen.

Mary was thrilled and thanked the villagers. To express her gratitude, she combed her hair and gave each villager a thousand pieces of gold. After John was released, Mary told him what the old lady had done. As Queen, Mary ordered some servants to dig a bottomless pit and put the old lady in it without food or water until she died. Mary was an honest and fair Queen. Due to her leadership, the village became the most prosperous village in the land and was the talk of all Kingdoms.

In Mankondelle, John and Mary's parents heard about a Queen with gifts, so they decided to go see for themselves. They took some bananas to sell on their way there to get some gold. When they arrived at the palace, they did not recognize John and Mary, but John and Mary knew who they were. Queen Mary sent one of her servants to buy all the bananas her parents were selling. After the servant bought the bananas, Queen Mary walked up to her parents and asked them the reason for their visit. After they told her, she invited them to come to a party at the palace in the evening. During the party, Queen Mary told the entire village her story and how her mother wanted to kill them for meat. The villagers were furious and stoned Mary's mother to death, but they welcomed her father to the village. A few years later, Mary married the hunter who had saved her life, and they lived happily ever after.

The end!

Moral of the story: A jealous heart is the shortest path to damnation.

Tales of The Wise Tortoise

Why the Tortoise has a Cracked Looking Shell

One upon a time, the Chief of Newendelle, organized a party in the sky for his daughter. She was the most beautiful girl in Newendelle, and this party was going to be remembered for centuries to come. Animals from all over the world were invited, but those without wings had to find a way to fly to the sky. Mr. Tortoise really wanted to attend the party, so he borrowed feathers from twelve birds. During the flight to the sky, Mr. Tortoise told the birds that he would change his name to "all of you" because he had obtained feathers from each one of them. The birds were thrilled and agreed to call Mr. Tortoise "all of you."

During the party, after the father and daughter dance, it was time for food. The servers took three trays of different types of food to the table where the Tortoise and birds were sitting and said, "This food is for all of you."

The birds were about to serve themselves when the Tortoise yelled, "WAIT, remember I changed my name to all of you, so this food is mine. I am sure the servers will come back with more food for you." The birds were a little concerned because they didn't know if Mr. Tortoise had told everyone at the party that he had changed his name, but they decided to wait for their own food. The birds angrily waited while Mr. Tortoise ate.

It was the end of the party, and no one had come back with more food for the birds, so they were furious and decided to take back the feathers they had given Mr. Tortoise. Mr. Tortoise tried to plead with the birds, but they refused to let him keep the feathers. He begged one of the birds to tell his wife to bring out all the soft things they had, like mattresses, pillows, etc., so that when he fell from the sky, he wouldn't hurt himself. When the bird arrived at Mr. Tortoise's house, she told Mrs. Tortoise that Mr. Tortoise wanted her to bring out all the sharp objects they had at home, like knives, spears, machetes, etc., because he was feeling brave and wanted to test his strength.

Mrs. Tortoise brought out all the sharp objects from the house. When Mr. Tortoise looked down from the sky and saw items on the ground, he assumed they were soft objects, so he jumped. He landed on all the sharp objects and cracked his smooth shell. Mr. Tortoise was in so much pain. It took months for his shell to heal, but it was never smooth again.

Moral of the story: Greed and selfishness leave permanent scars.

Why Pigs dig into the Ground

Once upon a time, there was a Tortoise and a Pig who were best friends. They did everything together, and their families were very close. Mr. Tortoise was going through some financial difficulties, so he asked Mr. Pig to lend him some gold. Mr. Pig agreed to lend Mr. Tortoise 5000 pieces of gold, and Mr. Tortoise agreed to pay him back in ten market days. When it was time for Mr. Tortoise to pay back the loan, Mr. Pig went to Mr. Tortoise's house to collect his gold. He met Mrs. Tortoise at home, who told him that Mr. Tortoise had gone on a journey and would be back the next day. Mr. Pig wished her goodnight and told her he would return the next day to collect his gold. Mr. Pig returned the next day, but Mrs. Tortoise told him that Mr. Tortoise had just left, so he should come back later in the evening. In the evening, when Mr. Tortoise heard Mr. Pig knocking on the door, he ran and hid. Mrs. Tortoise opened the door and told Mr. Pig that Mr. Tortoise wasn't back yet. This occurred for over a month, so Mr. Pig was losing his patience.

One Sunday, Mr. Pig went to Mr. Tortoise's house unannounced. Mrs. Tortoise was in the kitchen cooking Achu *(The traditional meal of some tribes in the NW region of Cameroon)* while Mr. Tortoise sat next to her. When Mr. Tortoise heard Mr. Pig walking towards the kitchen, he asked his wife to pretend to use him as a grinding stone because he didn't have enough time to hide.

Mr. Pig stomped into the kitchen and demanded to see Mr. Tortoise or else he would destroy everything in the house. Mrs. Tortoise's while using Mr. Tortoise as a grinding stone, told Mr. Pig that her husband had gone out and would not be back until later in the evening. Haven heard this story multiple times, Mr. Pig angrily took Mrs. Tortoise's grinding stone, which was Mr. Tortoise, and threw it out the window. Mrs. Tortoise started crying, and a few minutes later, Mr. Tortoise walked into the house and asked his wife why she was crying. She told him what had happened, and Mr. Tortoise started yelling at Mr. Pig. Mr. Pig told Mr. Tortoise that all he wanted was his gold, and once he received it, he would never speak to the Tortoise family again. Mr. Tortoise told Mr. Pig that he was not going to pay him back unless he found his wife's grinding stone. He also said that he wanted the same grinding stone, not a new one. Mr. Pig, not knowing that he had been tricked, left to fetch the stone. He dug and dug but couldn't find the stone, so he continued digging.

And this is why pigs are always digging into the ground.

Moral of the story: You can dig forever and never find the gold you lend to a trickster.

The Tortoise
and the Dog

Once upon a time, the Tortoise and Dog were good friends, but they were very competitive. The Dog was regarded as a superior animal because it had a way with humans and ran very fast. The Tortoise, on the other hand, was considered to be a slow animal who had nothing to offer. One day the Tortoise overhead the Dog, mocking him and laughing at how slow he walked. This angered the Tortoise, and given his competitive nature, he walked up to the Dog and challenged him to a race. The other animals laughed and didn't take the Tortoise seriously. The Tortoise ignored them and told the Dog that the first person who arrived at the King's palace from the market would win the race. The Dog laughed and agreed to do the race. The Tortoise said the race would start the next day at 6 a.m. The Dog laughed again and told the Tortoise to start at 6 a.m., but he would start at 8 a.m. to give the Tortoise's slow legs a head start. The Tortoise went home and thought of a strategy to win the race. He decided that if he wanted to win the race, he had to tempt the Dog with something he could not resist. Dogs have been known to love meat and bones, so the Tortoise went to the market and bought the finest meat and bones he could find. He took the meat and bones and put them along the road where the race was to occur. He put a little close to the market and increased the quantity as he proceeded towards the palace. There was a little meat near the market and a lot of meat close to the King's palace.

The next day, the Tortoise woke up and started the race promptly at 6 a.m., while the Dog slept and started at 8 a.m. As the Dog was running, he saw the meat and bones along the road, but he resisted them and continued running. He passed the Tortoise on the road and laughed at him, telling the Tortoise that he could never win even with a two-hour head start. The Tortoise ignored the Dog and continued running as fast as he could. When the Dog was about ten minutes away from the palace, he saw the massive pile of meat. He could not resist, so he stopped and ate until he could eat no more. Still confident that he would win, he decided to take a little nap before continuing. While he was sleeping, the Tortoise passed him.

When the Dog woke up, he saw the Tortoise about to cross the finish line, so he ran as fast as he could, but he could not catch up. The other animals were all waiting at the palace and cheered the Tortoise as he crossed the finish line. The race became the talk of the Kingdom, and the Dog lost his status in the Kingdom while the Tortoise was praised for his diligence and wisdom.

Moral of the story: Do not be too prideful and look down on others because the tables could turn when you least expect it.

The Lion and the Tortoise

One upon a time in the Kingdom of Acorndelle, there was a Fon *(a traditional ruler of a tribe)* who had the most beautiful daughter in the land. She had a huge mane and gorgeous brown eyes. Every suitor in the Kingdom wanted to marry her.

The Fon was very wealthy and had many farms and animals, but he had one problem. There was a Lion who repeatedly came to his farms at night and killed his animals. This kept the Fon up at night because he was losing so many assets daily. One morning during a palace meeting, the Fon announced that the animal who caught the Lion would marry his daughter. When the Tortoise heard this, he was intrigued and announced to the other animals that he would capture the Lion and marry the Fon's daughter. The other animals laughed at him and said, a small powerless animal like him would not stand a chance against the mighty Lion. Their mockery did not discourage the Tortoise. He went home, got a basket, went out to the field, and filled the basket with stones. He kept the basket of stones, waiting for the right moment to unleash his master plan.

One day, it started raining like it had never rained before, and the Kingdom was in complete darkness. Everyone in the Kingdom was afraid because they thought the earth would collide with the moon and it would be the end of the world.

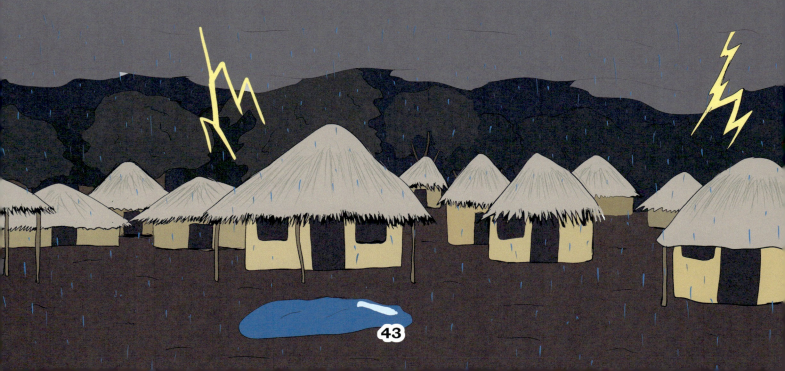

The Tortoise, on the other hand, saw this as an opportunity to unleash his plan to capture the Lion and marry the Fon's daughter, so he carried the basket filled with stones to the Lion's den. When he got there, the Lion was about to devour him, but he pleaded with the Lion saying that he had a plan which could save them both as the world was coming to an end. The Tortoise told the Lion that he was carrying all his children in the basket on his back and had dug a deep hole to put them inside so that they would be safe. He offered to go put his children in the hole and come back for the Lion, on condition that the Lion would offer him protection when the storm was over. The Lion was grateful and accepted the offer. The Tortoise left, walked a few miles away from the Lion's den, dumped the stones, then returned for the Lion. The Lion wanted to walk, but the Tortoise said that it was only appropriate that he carried him in the basket because, after all, the Lion was the King of the jungle. The Lion loved the royal reference and treatment, so he accepted and got into the basket, and the Tortoise tied the basket tightly.

Instead of going to put the Lion in the hole, the Tortoise carried the Lion towards the palace. When he got close to the palace, he started shouting and saying that he had captured the Lion, so all the animals in the Kingdom went to the palace to see for themselves. They were all shocked. The Fon, being a man of his words, thanked the Tortoise and said he could marry his daughter. The Tortoise was overjoyed but told the Fon that his only request was that they should not untie the Lion until he had gone far away with his bride because he was afraid that the Lion would come after him. The Fon agreed. When the Tortoise left with the Fon's daughter, the Chindas *(a palace servant or guard)* untied the Lion to punish him, but the Lion escaped and started chasing the Tortoise.

The Tortoise saw the Lion coming from a distance, and he knew exactly what was going to happen to him, so he started digging a hole as quickly as he could. When he had dug a deep enough hole, he got into the hole and pulled his bride inside, and then he used mud to cover the hole's entrance. The Lion searched the entire area, but he could not find the Tortoise.

That is how the Tortoise escaped to another Kingdom and lived happily ever after with his bride.

Moral of the story: Never underestimate someone because they are small. The real power lies in how we use our brains to see opportunities that no one else does.

The Race in the Animal Kingdom

Once upon a time, there was a feast in the Animal Kingdom. During the feast, the Queen announced that there would be a running competition. To win the competition, you had to be the first person to sit on the throne, and the prize for winning was 1200 pieces of gold. The Tortoise, being very competitive and proud, announced that he was going to win the race. All the animals present laughed at him and said that he couldn't even cross the road quickly, let alone win a race. The animal's mockery didn't derail the Tortoise. He left the feast confident in his ability to win. On the day of the race, all the animals lined up, and the Tortoise made sure he stood next to Cheetah, who was the fastest animal in the Kingdom. When the race began, the tiny Tortoise clung to the Cheetah's tail as he took off.

The Cheetah was extremely fast, so he was miles ahead of the other animals; thus, they couldn't see the Tortoise on the Cheetah's tail. The other animals continued to mock the Tortoise during the race because they assumed that he was far behind them since they couldn't see him. As the Cheetah arrived the finish line, the crowd cheered. When the Cheetah was about to sit on the throne, the Tortoise, hanging on his tail, sat on the throne first and screamed from underneath, "Please do not sit on me." To everyone's surprise, the Tortoise had won the race because he was the first animal to sit on the throne. All the animals in the Kingdom were in awe. The Tortoise took the 1200 pieces of gold from the Queen and walked away with his head held high.

Moral of the story: Never challenge the clever; all battles are battles of wits.

The Tortoise and the Poop

Once upon a time, there was a dance in the palace of Brennedelle. All the animals in the Kingdom were invited. The palace servants and chindas spent an entire week decorating, cooking, and preparing for the dance. The day before the dance, when everyone had gone to sleep, the Tortoise sneaked past the guards and pooped in the palace yard. After he pooped, he told the Poop that it should say the Elephant pooped it when asked who pooped it. The next day during the dance, when some animals were dancing towards the throne, the Tortoise joined them. When the Tortoise was dancing, he made sure he stepped on the Poop.

As the Tortoise stepped on the Poop, he screamed and told everyone to stop dancing because someone has committed an abomination. The drummers and musicians stopped the music, and everyone stopped dancing. The Fon was furious and said that whoever pooped in the yard would be killed and eaten by everyone for dinner. When the Fon said this, the Tortoise suggested that they should beat the Poop and ask who pooped it to find the culprit. The Fon and all the animals agreed, so they started beating the Poop and asking it who pooped it. After a few minutes of beating, the Poop confessed that the Elephant pooped it.

After the Poop confessed, the animals caught the Elephant, killed him, then ate him as part of the feast. The Tortoise was content because a couple of days earlier, the Elephant had stomped on his farm and destroyed all his crops.

Moral of the story: Be careful where you step. Those you trample on may get their revenge.

The Elephant, the Hippopotamus and the Tortoise

Once upon a time in the Animal Kingdom, the Elephant and the Hippopotamus were best friends, and they hated the Tortoise. They always mocked him and mistreated him. One day, when the animals in the Kingdom were bragging about how strong they were, the Tortoise said he was the strongest animal in the land. When he said this, the Elephant and Hippopotamus laughed so hard that the Elephant cried.

The Tortoise decided to teach the Elephant and the Hippopotamus a lesson, so he went to the Hippopotamus and challenged him to a tug-of-war battle to prove his strength. They agreed that the animal who lasted the longest would win the battle. The Tortoise then went to the Elephant and challenged him too. Unbeknown to the Elephant and Hippopotamus, they were going to be battling each other.

On the day of the battle the Tortoise went to the Elephant and tied a rope on his trunk. He told the Elephant that when he felt the rope move, he should know that the battle has begun, so he should start pulling. Then the Tortoise went to the Hippopotamus, gave him the other end of the rope, and told him the same thing he had told the Elephant. The Elephant and Hippopotamus didn't ask any questions, and they were not suspicious because they were confident that they were going to win against the Tortoise. The battle's location made it impossible for the Hippopotamus to see the Elephant, so they both assumed they were battling the Tortoise. When everything was ready, the Tortoise went to the middle and pulled the rope. Once the Elephant felt the rope move, he started pulling, so the Hippopotamus felt the rope move and pulled as well. The Tortoise stood in the middle and watched the Elephant and the Hippopotamus pull and pull.

After pulling for hours, one of the Hippopotamus's teeth fell out, and the Elephant's trunk almost cut, so they both decided to give up. After they gave up, the Tortoise went to them separately and said, "now who is the strongest animal in the land"?

The Elephant and Hippopotamus never realized that they had been tricked, and from that day on, they respected the Tortoise. Even though they were best friends, they were ashamed to tell each other what happened, so the Tortoise got away with it.

Moral of the story: It only takes brains to pull a rope

The Tortoise and the Spicy Food Competition

In the Kingdom of Spiceland, the Queen always hosted parties with different competitions. The animals looked forward to these parties because they always won priceless gifts and upgraded their status in Spiceland. One day the Queen announced that she was going to host an all-you-can-eat, spicy food competition. The winner would be the person who ate the biggest plate of spicy food without making the sound "ssssss."

The Dog, Elephant, Tiger, Monkey, Black Panther, and more came and tried to eat the spicy food, but they couldn't finish the plate without making the sound, "ssssss". When it was the Tortoise's turn, he sat down and started eating and singing, "Dog go make ssssss, but me I no go make ssssss." He sang this song until he finished the plate of food while calling the names of all the animals who had tried before him and failed.

When the Tortoise finished the big plate of spicy food, the Queen gave him four bags of gold, three bags of rhodium, and a bag of pearls. He was also named the only animal in the land who can handle the spice.

Moral of the story: A song is all you need to handle the spice

Other Tales

The Devil's land

Once upon a time, there lived two neighbors Richard and Ricky, who were the most successful garden egg farmers in Booboodelle. They were very wealthy and highly regarded by everyone in Booboodelle because the species of garden eggs that they grew were very rare.

One year, Ricky's garden eggs did not do well. He lost most of his wealth and couldn't afford to buy food for his family, so he went to Richard's farm and stole some garden eggs for his wife to cook. Later in the evening, when Richard went to visit Ricky, he caught Ricky and his family eating the garden eggs.

Richard was furious and told Ricky that he had 10 days to pay him back with the exact species of garden eggs or else he would report him to the King. Ricky went around Booboodelle, looking for that species of garden egg, but no one had it. One day, when Ricky was at the market square, a fruit seller told him that he could find that species of garden eggs in the Devil's land, but they eat humans there. Ricky had no choice, so he decided to go to the Devil's land. On his way there, he met an old lady struggling to clear her farm, and she begged him to help her.

Ricky agreed to help the old lady, and when he was done, she asked him where he was going. He told her that he was going to the Devil's land to look for a rare species of garden eggs. The old lady decided to give Ricky her machete to thank him.

As Ricky continued his journey, he came across some cattlemen trying to catch their cows that had escaped, so he decided to stop and help them.

When Ricky finished helping the cattlemen, they thanked him and asked him where he was going. He told them. The cattlemen told him that they didn't have any money to offer him, but they could offer him some corn for his journey. Ricky took the corn, thanked the cattlemen, and continued to the Devil's land.

After three days of walking, he arrived at the Devil's land. He saw the rare garden eggs and was about to harvest them when three little devils came out of the bushes and surrounded him.

They asked him what he was doing in the Devil's land, and he told them his story. The three little Devils laughed and said, "No human has ever left the Devil's land alive. We are going to kill you and eat you". The Devils had giant chickens, which they used as guards, so they ordered four of the chickens to capture Ricky and put him in a cage.

While in the cage, Ricky took out the corn that the cattlemen had given him and threw it far away.

The chickens loved corn, so they all ran in the direction of the corn and started eating it. While the chickens were eating the corn, Ricky used the matchet to free himself and harvested many garden eggs.

Before he ran away, he stole some of the Devil's money. When he got back to Booboodelle, everyone was surprised and happy because no one had ever returned from the Devil's land. The next day, Ricky went to Richard's house and repaid him the garden eggs he had stolen from his farm. With the garden eggs and money Ricky had stolen from the Devils, he became the richest man in Booboodelle, even richer than the King. Richard became extremely jealous of Ricky, so he decided to go to the Devil's land in search of riches. He packed a bag full of food, weapons, and everything he thought he would need then, left for the Devil's land in the middle of the night.

On Richard's way to the Devil's land, he met the same old lady Ricky had met. The old lady begged him to help her clear her farm, but he insulted her and said that he didn't have time because he was on a very important mission. As he continued his journey, he met the cattlemen trying to catch their cows that had escaped. Richard passed by and acted like he didn't see them struggling.

When he arrived the Devil's land, he saw the garden eggs and started cutting them and singing, *"This place smells, this place smells, this place smells like the devil's land."* When the Devils heard him singing, they all came out and ate him immediately because they were furious that one human had escaped before.

Moral of the story: Be kind to everyone you come across; you never know who might offer you something that would save your life.

The Sultan's Daughter

Once upon a time, there was a very wealthy Sultan in the Kingdom of Jabarta. The Sultan and his wife had been married for many years. They had everything they wanted except a child. One day the Sultan's wife started feeling sick, so she went to the hospital and found out she was pregnant. She was overjoyed and could not wait to tell her husband. On her way home, she stopped at the market to get some groceries. When she was shopping, an old man came up to her and said, "Young lady, are you with child because your joy is radiating throughout the market square." She smiled and said, "Yes, I am. I have tried for many, many years, and my prayers have finally been answered." The old man told her to raise her child with love but not give her everything she wants. She smiled and thanked him.

On her way home, she wondered how the old man knew she would have a girl. When she got home, she told the Sultan the good news. He was so happy that he threw the biggest party Jabarta had ever seen. When the Sultan's wife gave birth, they named their daughter Olujimi which means God's gift. Olujimi had everything she wanted, but she didn't treat the people who took care of her nicely. Her parents did nothing because she was their only child and meant everything to them.

As Olujimi grew older, her behavior got worse. News of her bad behavior spread across Jabarta, so no man wanted to marry her. Her parents decided to throw parties each month and invited every eligible suitor in Jabarta, hoping that one of them would be interested in Olujimi and eventually ask for her hand in marriage. During these parties, Olujimi was rude to the guests and disrespected them, so no man ever asked for her hand in marriage.

As Olujimi grew older, the Sultan and his wife were worried because nothing they had tried worked, and Olujimi had no friends or suitors. One day while Olujimi's mother was reading in her garden, she had an idea. People in the faraway lands do not know anything about her daughter's behavior, so what if she organized a party and invited just suitors from other lands. She brought this up to her husband, and he agreed to give it a try.

On the day of the party, suitors from respectable families and professions came and tried to win Olujimi's hand in marriage. The Prince from the North came and sang, *"I am a handsome Prince who comes from the North, who comes from the North just to marry you, oh will you marry, marry, marry, will you marry me."*

After the Prince finished singing, Olujimi sang, *"You are a very handsome Prince who comes from the North, who comes from the North just to marry me, oh I won't marry, marry, marry, I won't marry you."* Doctors, Engineers, Farmers, Kings, Princes, and more came and sang, but Olujimi's response was the same. She rejected all of them.

Her parents were confused and asked her why she rejected all the suitors. She said she wasn't interested in their status or who they were as people. All she was interested in was money because she has always had money and everything she wanted, so she would not marry a man who didn't offer her money. Her parents were shocked by her response, and immediately her mother remembered what the old man had told her in the market a long time ago, and she started weeping. The Sultan asked his wife why she was crying, and all she said was, this is my fault I should have listened to the old man. The Sultan was confused and was asking what she meant when a servant walked in and told them that another suitor just arrived, so they went back to the party. The suitor walked in and started singing, *"I give to you all my money, all my money just to marry you oh will you marry, marry, marry, will you marry me?"*

Once Olujimi heard this, she was overjoyed and sang. *"You give to me all your money, all your money just to marry me oh, I will marry, marry, marry, I will marry you."* Then the suitor sang, *"Oh ha ha ha, you look so funny, you love my money, but you don't love me oh I won't marry, marry, marry, I won't marry you."*

After the suitor sang, he took all his money and left. Olujimi and her parents were shocked. Olujimi never married or had any friends and continued to live in her parents' house until she died.

Moral of the story: Too much wealth may compromise your heart

The Greatest Hunter in Lumisdelle

Once upon a time, there was a beast terrorizing Lumisdelle. The people of Lumisdelle lived in fear because the creature had killed their children and livestock. No one had ever seen this beast because it attacked at night. All the villagers knew was that when the beast grabbed a child or an animal, it took them in the direction of the evil forest, where no man had ever gone. The King of Lumisdelle gathered all the villagers together because the situation was getting out of hand. He told them that whoever captured the beast, dead or alive, would marry his favorite daughter. Maghah, the greatest hunter in the land, stood up and promised the King that he would kill the beast. The King thanked him. Maghah went home, gathered all his spears, machetes and traps, and set out for the evil forest. Fortunately for Maghah, he came across the beast when it had just eaten and was asleep.

Instead of killing the beast, he decided to wait for it to wake up. He told himself that a brave and mighty hunter like him cannot kill a sleeping animal. Maghah was a man who loved attention and praise, so while waiting for the beast to wake up, he ran back to Lumisdelle and told everyone to come to the evil forest and watch him kill the beast, so that they would tell the story for generations to come. All the villagers, including the King, followed Maghah to the evil forest. They took torches, spears, and everything they could find. When the villagers arrived where the beast was sleeping, they started chanting; *today na your last day for this ground.* Their chant awakened the beast. It let out a mighty roar which made Maghah and the villagers panic. Their moment of panic allowed the beast to escape.

The story became the talk of Lumisdelle, and Maghah went from being the bravest to the stupidest hunter in the land. That same night, while the villagers were asleep, the beast struck again. This time it took the King's favorite pet, a German Shepherd named Justice. The King was furious and blamed Maghah, so he exiled Maghah from Lumisdelle. As Maghah was crossing Lumisdelle's border, his eldest son Fru placed his hand on his shoulder and said, "Father, I will finish what you started."

After Maghah left, Fru his eldest son set out for the evil forest to find the beast and kill it. He searched the forest for 22 days and was about to give up when he climbed a mango tree to harvest some mangoes and spotted the beast below him. He waited for the right moment and then pounced on the beast with his spear.

The beast was severely wounded it continued fighting. After about 40 minutes of fighting, Fru killed the beast. He carried the beast on his shoulder and set out for Lumisdelle. When some Chindas *(a palace guard or servant)* saw Fru approaching Lumisdelle with the beast on his shoulder, they were overjoyed and immediately ran to the palace and started sounding the drums and agogos.

The sound they played was a message calling every citizen of Lumisdelle to the palace. When everyone was gathered at the palace, Fru presented the beast to the King and said, "My King, I present to you the beast that has been terrorizing our land, and from this day on, peace shall reign in Lumisdelle."

The King was pleased. As promised, Fru was allowed to marry the King's favorite daughter. Instead of marrying the King's daughter, Fru pleaded with the King to forgive his father so that he could return to Lumisdelle. The King granted his request, so Fru went and brought his father back to Lumisdelle. Maghah was so happy to be back, and his family threw a huge party to welcome him home.

During the party, the King walked into Fru's house, and everyone was stood still because they were in shock. The King told everyone not to worry because he came bearing good news. He announced that because Fru had been so courageous and chose to have his father come back instead of marrying his daughter, he would like Fru to still marry his daughter only if Fru wanted to. Fru was so happy and thanked the King. He got married to the princess, and they lived happily ever after.

Moral of the story: Never let your ego get the best of you like Maghah the hunter, and sometimes we have to make sacrifices for the people we love like Fru.

Why Women are Celebrated in Mankon

Once upon a time, there was a couple who lived with their families in the same house so, they barely had any personal time. After three years of dating, the couple decided to get married. A few weeks before their wedding, they bought a house and decided to move in on their wedding night. They made a promise to each other that on their wedding night, they would be alone no matter what.

They had a simple, elegant wedding and went back to their new home to start their honeymoon. They had their home decorated with roses, hibiscus, and sunflowers. They also lit multiple midnight glow candles and played zouk music. Right when they were about to settle in and spend some quality time together, someone knocked on the door. It was the groom's parents. His wife reminded him of their promise, so he went and sent his parents away without listening to what they wanted. A few minutes later, there was another knock on the door. This time it was the bride's parents. Her husband reminded her of their promise, but his wife couldn't just send her parents away, because what if it was an emergency. She decided to open the door. Her parents told her that they came to get her mother's diabetes medication that she had forgotten when decorating the couple's new home. Her mother grabbed her medication, thanked her daughter for opening the door, and left.

A year later, the wife gave birth to a bouncing baby boy. Her husband and the whole family were overjoyed and celebrated. Two years later, the wife gave birth to another boy, and the entire family celebrated. One year later, the wife gave birth to a baby girl, and her husband was happier than she had ever seen. He invited family and friends from around the globe to celebrate the birth of his baby girl and threw a big party. His wife was perplexed, so she asked him, "Why didn't you throw a big party when our sons were born?" He responded, "Because my baby girl would be the one to open the door for me like you opened the door for your parents on our wedding night."

Moral of the story: A rule is never more important than a person in need.

Glossary

Agogos	A samba instrument with one or multiple bells used across African and Latin cultures
Cornrow	Cornrow is a style of hair braiding in which the hair is braided very close to the scalp, using an underhand, upward motion to make a continuous, raised row.)
Chindas	A palace servant or guard
Chief	A ruler of a village
Fon	A ruler of a tribe
Fufu corn and NjamaNjama	A common meal in the Northwest Region of Cameroon - (The traditional food of the Nso people)
Garden Egg	A type of eggplant that is eaten across Africa
Hunter Man	A hunter
Jollof rice	A popular rice dish eaten across many West African countries
Mankon	A tribe in the Northwest Region of Cameroon

Printed in the United States
By Bookmasters